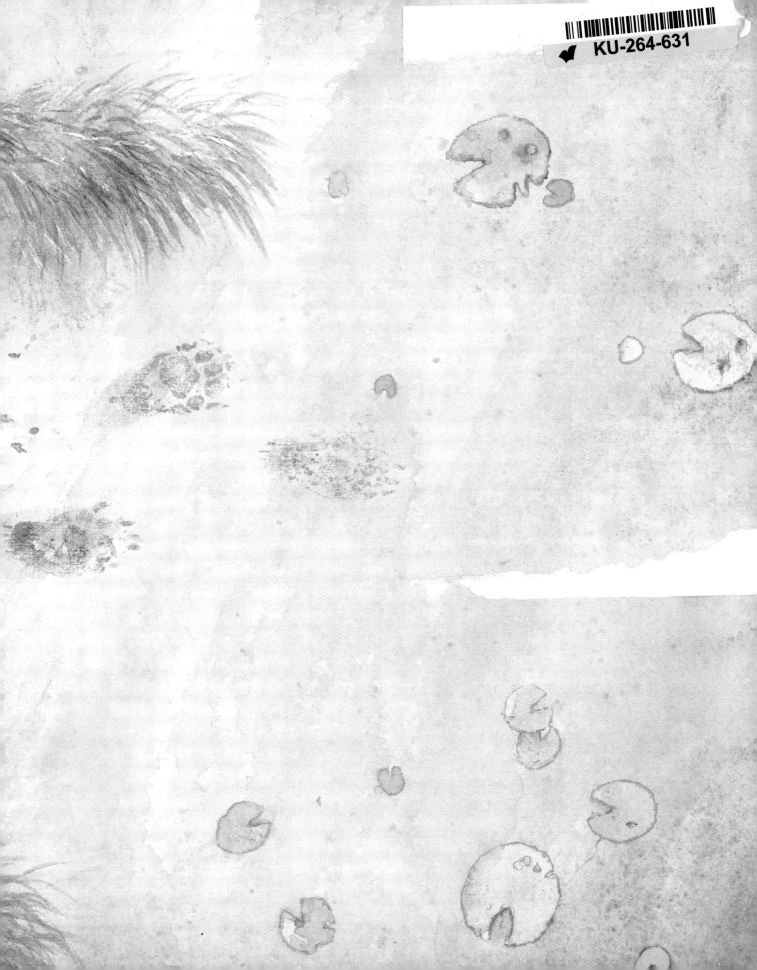

Bear's Eggs

Ingrid and Dieter Schubert

Andersen Press • London

One morning, when Bear walked to the lake, he found three eggs. He looked around. "Hello?" he shouted. Nobody answered. Bear waited and waited and no one came. At last he carefully picked up the eggs. "I won't leave you here alone," he said.

On his way home he met Hedgehog. "What's that you're
holding?" he asked.

Proudly Bear showed him the eggs. "I'm looking after them."

Hedgehog shook his head. "They'll need a nest, you know."

"Then I'll build one," Bear said. And he carried the eggs
to his cave, picked some grass, and made a nest.

"That's not enough," said Hedgehog. "They have to be kept warm, so you have to sit on them. Shall I show you how?"

"No!" Bear cried. "You're too prickly. I'm soft and warm."

Hedgehog sighed and walked away.

Bear lay down on the nest, being very careful of the eggs, and fell asleep.

Bear woke with a start. Something had pricked his
stomach! He jumped up.

Three little chicks looked at him, tweeting softly.

"Hedgehog!" Bear shouted, and Hedgehog came running.

"Well," Hedgehog said, "that's what happens."

"What do I do now?" Bear asked.

"Feed them and protect them and raise them ..."

"I can do that," Bear said.

"... and teach them to swim," Hedgehog continued.

"I can't do *that!*" Bear whispered. "It's too embarrassing."

"That's your problem," Hedgehog said. "I have to go
home now."

Deep in thought, Bear looked at the chicks. "Do you want
some honey? Brambles?"

The three chicks just looked at him.

There was no getting round it. Bear headed for the lake.
When he got there, Bear threw himself into the water.
Peeping loudly, the chicks stayed on the bank.

"Hedgehog!" Bear cried.
Hedgehog was there in a flash.
"They don't want to swim," Bear said.
"You're too wild. You have to carry them."
Bear grumbled and swam very gently with the chicks
on his back. One after another they jumped into the water and
paddled close to him.
"Ha!" Bear laughed proudly. "I taught them that."

"Now you have to get them something to eat,"
called Hedgehog.

Bear climbed on top of a rock and looked into the water.
Suddenly he swung his paw and caught a fish.

Quickly the chicks swam away.

"They're not hungry," Bear said, disappointed.

Hedgehog laughed. "That fish is much too big. You need
to get some small fish for them."

Bear took a deep breath and dived. The chicks followed him and, sure enough, they ate. Bear was very impressed.

Day in, day out, Bear took care of the chicks. He woke up with them and he went to sleep with them.

They played together and Bear protected them.

Then one day the chicks stood in front of Bear and flapped
their wings.

"Hedgehog!" Bear called.

Hedgehog sauntered by.

"Why are they doing that?" Bear asked.

"They want to learn to fly. They're young geese, and geese
fly!"

Bear shook his head. "Oh boy, flying is something I *really*
can't do."

Hedgehog rubbed his nose. "You've got to try. I'll help you."

Together they walked to the top of a high hill. "Now run down and flap your arms," said Hedgehog.

"Do you think that will help?" Bear asked.

Hedgehog nodded. "Absolutely."

Bear ran down the hill, flapping his arms wildly. The young geese followed him on foot, over and over and over again.

"Why don't you fly?" Bear panted. The baby geese tweeted softly but remained firmly on the ground.

Bear was desperate and Hedgehog was at his wits' end. Suddenly Bear said, "I've got an idea."

He placed the goslings on his shoulders and climbed
a high tree. Then Bear closed his eyes tightly, counted to three,
and jumped. Hedgehog held his breath. With a loud splash
Bear landed in the water.

All in a flurry, the geese flapped their wings and, lo and behold,
they were flying!

Hedgehog patted Bear on the back. "I'm proud of you. They couldn't have done it without you."

Bear collapsed on the grass. "Never again," he muttered, "never again."

Suddenly a little voice next to him squeaked softly, "Can you teach us to fly too?"

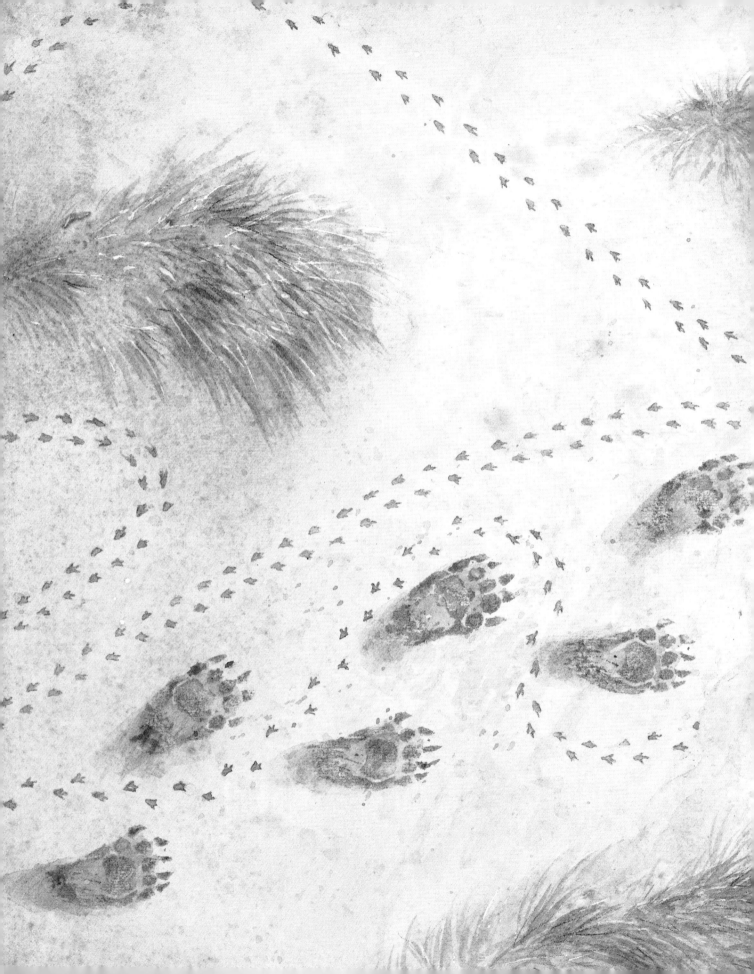